Ten-Gallon Bart and the WILD WEST SHOW

by **Susan Stevens Crummel**

illustrated by **Dorothy Donohue**

Marshall Cavendish Children

Ten-Gallon Bart used to be sheriff. Sheriff of Dog City. Then he retired so he could sleep until noon, howl at the moon, and go fishing anytime he wanted. But now he was plumb tired of sleeping, plumb tired of howling, and plumb tired of fishing. In fact, he was plumb tired of being retired.

Bart moseyed into Miss Kitty's Place.

"Why the long face?" purred Miss Kitty.

Bart sighed. "I'm bored. Same old thing every day. Sleepin', howlin', and fishin'.
I need to do somethin' diff'rent. Somethin' excitin'. Somethin'—"

"Wild and woolly?" interrupted Buffalo Gal. "I just got this poster from my brother, Chip. He's bringin' his Wild West Show to Dog City."

"Buffalo Chip's Wild West Show!" yelled Bart. "Well, I'll be doggone!"

Buffalo Chip's
WILD WEST SHOW

Coming to Dog City
Saturday
Trick Riding
Trick Roping
Trick Seed-spitting

Bring the
whole family!
BULL RIDING
Lots of fun

"Hey, look!" Bart cried. "There's a ridin' contest. I could be a star! Yippee! Remember that ol' goat Billy the Kid? He was B-A-A-A-D. And I rode the meanness right outta him. Nothin' to it!"

"Hold your horses," warned Miss Kitty. "This is a bull-ridin' contest, not a goat-ridin' contest. I heard Crazy Bull's the biggest, wildest, orneriest, fiercest—"

"Laziest bull around," interrupted Buffalo Gal. "Seen it with my own eyes. He sleeps all day! They should call it a bull-dozin' contest. But when he wakes up, wOO-WEE! He goes from Lazy Bull to Crazy Bull! Problem is, nobody can wake 'im, much less ride 'im."

"Hmmmm. Wakin' up a bull," pondered Bart. "Anyone got any ideas?"

WILD STAR OF THE
WEST SHOW!

"Crowin'!" chirped Miss Pixie. "That's what wakes me up every mornin'. Just COCK-A-DOODLE-DOO right in his ear. I know he'll wake up."

"The smell of food,"
grunted Wyatt Burp. "That's what wakes me up every mornin'.
Just hold some food right in front of his nose. I know he'll wake up."

"Kittens pullin' my tail," hissed Miss Kitty.
"That's what wakes me up every mornin'.
Just pull his tail. I know he'll wake up."

Bart's head was spinning. "Me, the star of a Wild West show!
My name in lights, my picture on posters. I'll be famous. How excitin'!
Crazy Bull, get ready for Ten-Gallon Bart!"

On Saturday Buffalo Chip's Wild West Show pulled
into Dog City. Everyone for miles around came to watch.
Hopalong Hare did some mighty fine turtle riding.
Calamity Cow did some mighty fine lasso roping.
Nannie Oakley did some mighty fine seed spitting.

The bull-riding contest was the grand finale.

Bart gasped as an enormous bull was hauled into the arena.

"Ladies and gentlemen!" Buffalo Chip announced in a booming voice. "Anyone who can wake up Crazy Bull and ride 'im will be the new star of my Wild West Show!"

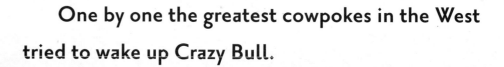

One by one the greatest cowpokes in the West
tried to wake up Crazy Bull.

Cat Carson,

Roy Rooster,

and Jesse Jackalope.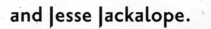

They pulled. They pushed.
They poked. They punched.
They prodded. They pleaded.

Nothing worked. No one could wake up that bull!

It was time for the last contestant.
A hush fell over the crowd.

Ten-Gallon Bart was as cool as a cucumber. He ambled up to Crazy Bull and crowed in his ear, **"COCK-A-DOODLE-DOO!"**

z-z-z-z-z-z-z

Z-z

Bart held some food in front of his nose.

z-z-Z-Z-Z-z-z

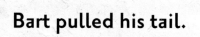

Bart pulled his tail.

The crowd
was restless.
"BOO-Oo-OO-Oo!
Give IT UP, BART!
IT'S OVER!
GO HOME!"

But Bart didn't want to go
home. He wanted to be famous.
He wanted to be the star of the
Wild West Show.

Then he saw it.
The blanket.
THE RED BLANKET.
Bart reached out.

YANK!

Crazy Bull opened his eyes.

BLiNK!

He flared his nostrils.

SNORT!

He leaped to his feet.

THUD!

Crazy Bull roared at the top of his lungs,

"My blankey! SOMEONE HAS STOLEN my blankey!"

Bart held out the blanket.

Crazy Bull tore out across the arena.

At the last second, Bart jerked up the blanket and hopped on.

Crazy Bull went crazy. Soaring. Roaring. Twisting.
Tossing. Turning. Churning up the ground with
every buck.

Bart hung on for dear life.

The crowd went wild.

"GO, BART!! RIDE 'IM, COWBOY!!!"

The buzzer rang just as Ten-Gallon Bart
and the blanket flew through the air,

WOOOOWEEE!

and landed in the dirt.

WHAM!

Crazy Bull grabbed
his blanket, lay down
in the arena,

and went back to sleep.

z-z-z-z-z-z-z-z

The crowd cheered as Buffalo Chip reached out his hand to Ten-Gallon Bart. "Best ride I've ever seen. Congratulations—you're the new star of my Wild West Show!"

"Thanks, but no thanks," Bart whimpered. "I've had all the wild and woolly excitement I can stand!"

"My blankey! SOMEONE HAS stOLEN my blankey!"

Ten-Gallon Bart retired for the second time.

But you won't find him fishing. And you won't find him howling.

You'll find him wrapped up warm and cozy in his special gift from Buffalo Chip
— the red blanket. z-z-z-z-z-z-z-z

And sometimes, if it's real quiet and the coyotes aren't yipping, you can hear
the sound of an enormous bull bellowing across the prairie,

"My blankey! SOMEONE HAS stOLEN my blankey!"

BAR

For the many cowboys and cowgirls in my family, past and present and future —S.S.C.

To Julia and Joe, our little stars, and the newest buckaroos, Connor, Ruby and Allijo —D.D.

Text copyright © 2008 by Susan Stevens Crummel
Illustrations copyright © 2008 by Dorothy Donohue

All rights reserved
Marshall Cavendish Corporation, 99 White Plains Road, Tarrytown, NY 10591
www.marshallcavendish.us/kids

Library of Congress Cataloging-in-Publication Data
Crummel, Susan Stevens.
Ten-Gallon Bart and the Wild West Show / by Susan Stevens Crummel; illustrated by Dorothy Donohue.
— 1st ed.
p. cm.
Summary: Buffalo Chip's Wild West Show comes to Dog City and retired sheriff Bart, looking for some
excitement, enters the bull-riding contest.
ISBN 978-0-7614-5391-8
[1. Dogs—Fiction. 2. Animals—Fiction. 3. Wild west shows—Fiction. 4. Bull riding—Fiction. 5. West
(U.S.)—Fiction.] I. Donohue, Dorothy, ill. II. Title.
PZ7.C88845Th 2008
[E]—dc22
2007011943

The text of this book is set in Priori San Bold.
The illustrations are rendered with textured papers, layered and pasted down.
Book design by Virginia Pope
Editor: Margery Cuyler

Printed in China
First edition
1 3 5 6 4 2

mc Marshall Cavendish
Children